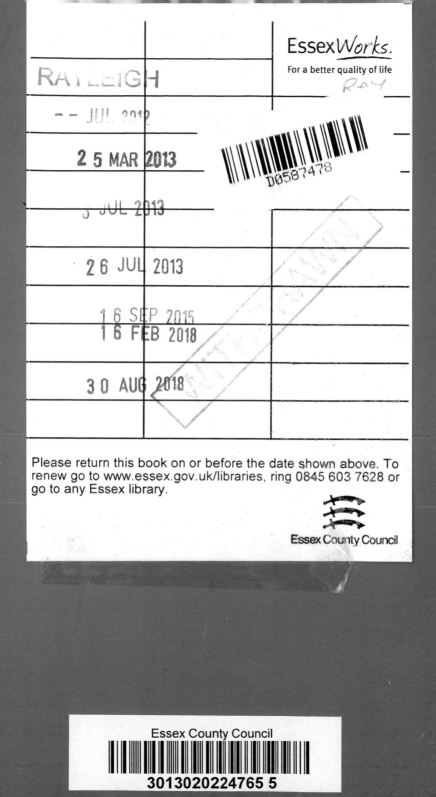

RATLEIGH

-- JUL 2012

2 5 MAR 2013

J JUL 2013

2 6 JUL 2013

1 6 SEP 2015

1 6 FEB 2018

3 0 AUG 2018

D0587478

EssexWorks.
For a better quality of life
RAY

Please return this book on or before the date shown above. To
renew go to www.essex.gov.uk/libraries, ring 0845 603 7628 or
go to any Essex library.

Essex County Council

Essex County Council

3013020224765 5

For Jake and Fleur Pirotta
S.P.

To my boys
J.L.

ORCHARD BOOKS
338 Euston Road, London NW1 3BH
Orchard Books Australia
Level 17/207 Kent Street, Sydney, NSW 2000
This text was first published in Great Britain
in the form of a gift collection called *First Greek Myths*, in 2003
First published in 2005 by Orchard Books
First published in paperback in 2006
ISBN 978 1 84362 783 8
Text © Saviour Pirotta 2005
Cover illustrations © Jan Lewis 2003
Inside illustrations © Jan Lewis 2005
The rights of Saviour Pirotta to be identified as the author and
Jan Lewis to be identified as the illustrator of this work
have been asserted by them in accordance with the
Copyright, Designs and Patents Act, 1988.
A CIP catalogue record for this book is available from the British Library.
10 9 8 7 6 5 4
Printed in China
Orchard Books is a division of Hachette Children's Books,
an Hachette UK company.
www.hachette.co.uk

~FIRST GREEK MYTHS~
ODYSSEUS AND THE WOODEN HORSE

BY SAVIOUR PIROTTA
ILLUSTRATED BY JAN LEWIS

ORCHARD BOOKS

~ CAST LIST ~

ODYSSEUS
(Odd-ee-see-us)

A brave and clever
Greek soldier

HELEN
(Hell-en)

A beautiful queen

Long ago in Greece there was a beautiful queen called Helen. She lived in a huge palace with maids to look after her and a king to adore her.

She should have been happy and content, but she wasn't. She fell in love with the handsome Paris, a prince from the city of Troy, and ran away with him.

The King sent a great army to
bring Helen back. Led by the brave
Odysseus, the soldiers surrounded
the city of Troy. But, try as they
might, they could not capture it.

After nine long years of fighting, the soldiers wanted to go home. But Odysseus wanted to try just one more time to enter the city – and he had a plan. He called together his generals.

Slowly, he opened a scroll and laid it out in front of them to see.

"A wooden horse on wheels?" bellowed an old general. "Are you mad? How will that help us beat the Trojans?"

"Look closely," said Odysseus, "and you will see that it is a giant, hollow horse. There is enough space inside it for fifty soldiers."

Odysseus lowered his voice. "I will hide inside the horse with my best soldiers," he whispered.

"Then, when the Trojans become curious and take the horse into the city, we can capture Queen Helen."

"It's risky," said the general.

But all the other men knew that Odysseus's plans usually worked.

"Well, it's worth a try, I suppose," said the general. "Start building it behind that hill, so the Trojans can't see you!"

In a week, the giant horse was ready.

When it got dark, Odysseus chose fifty of his bravest men and they all hid inside the horse. The other soldiers wheeled it to the gates of Troy.

All through the night, no one inside the horse dared to move, in case they made a noise.

At last a cock crowed. It was morning. Just outside, Odysseus could hear the Trojans talking.

"Look! The Greeks have left.
They have given up on capturing
Queen Helen and gone home!"
    Then someone said, "But they've
left a giant wooden horse
behind!"

"Quick! Bring it into the city," someone shouted. "Then we can have a closer look at it."

"NO!" called someone else. "It could be a trick. Push it over the cliffs into the sea!"

Odysseus and his men held
their breath and tried to keep
calm. The wooden horse started
to move.

The Trojans were pulling it along on its wheels, but which way was it going? Into the city or over the cliff...?

Odysseus knew how scared his men were, but he didn't dare say anything to make them feel better in case the Trojans heard him.

At last, the horse stopped moving. Odysseus and his men could hear music and singing. The Trojans were celebrating their victory over the Greeks. For hours the beating of drums echoed.

Then, gradually, the noise
stopped and everything went quiet.

"Are we in the city or on the cliffs?" whispered one of Odysseus's soldiers.

Carefully, Odysseus opened the trap door in the horse's tummy and peered out.

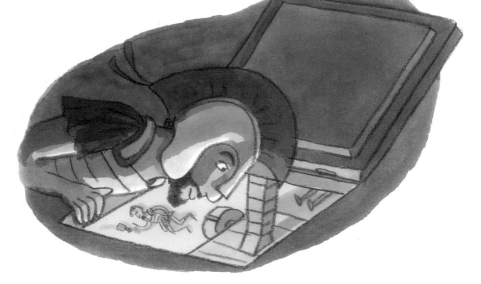

He saw a few young men lying fast asleep on the paved ground, with wine cups in their hands.

"We're in the city," he whispered. "Follow me!"

One by one the soldiers climbed down a ladder to the ground.

They followed Odysseus
through the narrow streets of
the city.

Here and there people
lay snoring in doorways.

The Trojans had celebrated until
they were so tired they fell asleep.

"We have to open the city gates
and let in the rest of our soldiers,"
said Odysseus.

Quietly, the Greek men made their way through the streets with their swords. At last, they saw the city gates up ahead. They also saw that one Trojan soldier was still on guard.

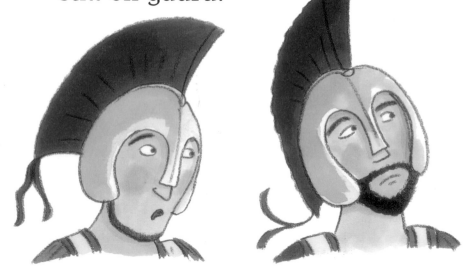

"He will raise the alarm if he sees us," one of the men said to Odysseus.

But as they drew closer and
closer to the gates, they could see
that the soldier was fast asleep
at his post.

Odysseus nodded to his men
and they removed the huge wooden
plank that held the gates shut. The
gates made a very loud creak.

The guard began to stir. The
Greek soldiers looked at each other.
Was he about to wake up?

But no, the guard simply changed
his position and continued to snore.

Slowly, the great gates of Troy swung open. Thousands of Greek soldiers poured into the city. They had captured Troy at last.

Queen Helen was taken back to Greece. In time, the King forgave her, and Odysseus was remembered as a hero for ever.

~FIRST GREEK MYTHS~

BY SAVIOUR PIROTTA ~ ILLUSTRATED BY JAN LEWIS

And enjoy a little magic with these First Fairy Tales:

Orchard Books are available from all good bookshops,
or can be ordered from our website: www.orchardbooks.co.uk,
or telephone 01235 827702, or fax 01235 827703